Hello, Baby Badger

A Red Fox Book

Published by Random House Children's Books
20 Vauxhall Bridge Road, London SW1V 2SA

A division of Random House UK Ltd
London Melbourne Sydney Auckland
Johannesburg and agencies throughout the world

© Ron Maris 1992

First published by Julia MacRae Books 1992
Red Fox edition 1994

Printed in Singapore

RANDOM HOUSE UK Limited Reg. No. 954009

J111,496   £4.99

Hello, Baby Badger

Ron Maris

Red Fox

"Hello, Baby Badger.

Are you going for a walk?"

"We'll all come with you."

"Hello, Baby Badger.
Are you going for a walk?"

"We'll all come with you."

"Hello, Baby Badger.
Are you going for a walk?"

"We'll all come with you."

"But what is this we've found?"

Jill, 496

"Be careful, Baby Badger!"

"Hello, Baby Badger!"

"What shall we do?

Baby Badger can't swim!"

"We'd better rescue him ...

... and take him home!"

"Hello, Baby Badger.
Have you been for a walk?"